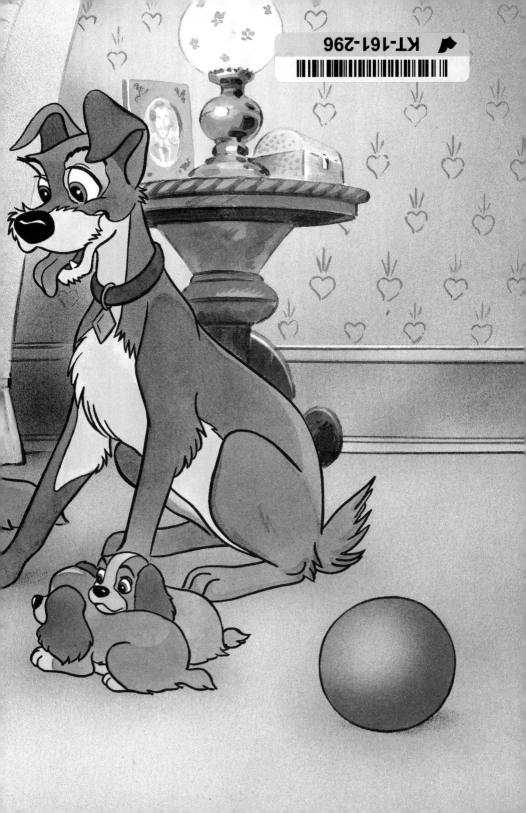

# WALT DISNEY'S

## *Lady* and the TRAMP

First American Edition.
Copyright © 1994 The Walt Disney
Company. All rights reserved under
international copyright conventions.
Published in the United States by Grolier
Enterprises Inc., Danbury, Connecticut.

Originally published in Denmark by
Egmont Books, Copenhagen, in 1993.

ISBN: 0–7172–8340–2
Manufactured in the United States.

A B C D           1 2 3 4

GROLIER
BOOK CLUB EDITION

Jim Dear and his wife, Darling, were celebrating
Christmas Eve.

"Here, Darling," he said, handing her a pretty box.

Darling untied the ribbon, and out popped the most
adorable cocker spaniel puppy she had ever seen.

"I love her," Darling exclaimed happily. "She's a
perfect little lady!"

When Lady was six months old, Darling and Jim
Dear gave her a brand-new collar and name tag.

"How fine you look in your new collar, Lady,"
Darling said.

That night, as usual, Jim Dear tucked Lady into
her very own basket.

Lady was the princess of the household. Jim Dear
and Darling loved to pamper her. They gave her special
treats from the table, and they always found time to
play with her. Lady was sure that she was the luckiest
dog in the whole wide world.

But as spring blossomed into summer, Jim Dear and Darling began to play with Lady less and less. Now, they spent most of their time talking about someone named "baby."

"Who is this 'baby'?" Lady asked herself.

"A baby is nothing but a bundle of trouble," said a husky voice. Lady whirled around to see who was speaking. It was a scruffy-looking dog she had never seen before. Why, he wasn't even wearing a collar!

"By the way, Pidge," he said, "my name is Tramp. What's yours?"

"I'm sorry," replied Lady, "but I never speak to strangers."

"Suit yourself," said Tramp. "But mark my words," he called out as he trotted away, "when a baby moves in, a dog moves out."

A short time later Lady heard new sounds coming from the master bedroom—soft, cooing sounds.

"Come in, Lady," Darling said gently. "There's someone I'd like you to meet."

"So this is what a baby looks like," thought Lady, wagging her tail happily. "He's not awful at all. Why, he's almost as sweet as a puppy!"

Soon life in Lady's household had almost returned to normal. But one day a stern-looking woman barged through the front door carrying a suitcase and a big basket.

"We're going away for a few days," Darling explained to Lady. "And we're counting on you to take good care of the baby. Aunt Sarah, here, has come to help you."

Two pairs of blue eyes stared at Lady from the basket. "I wonder what she has in there," said Lady.

She soon found out!
The eyes belonged to
Aunt Sarah's cats,
Si and Am.

The two cats hopped
out of the basket and
made themselves
at home.

"We are Siamese,
if you please! We are
Siamese, if you don't
please!" they hissed.

Lady got the feeling that Si and Am didn't like her. And for some reason, Aunt Sarah didn't seem too friendly, either. Lady watched sadly as Darling and Jim Dear walked out the door.

"Oh, please don't leave me here alone," she said softly.

Aunt Sarah went upstairs to check on the baby. As soon as the mischievous cats saw her leave, they began to turn the house upside down!

"Stop that!" Lady barked angrily. She really had her paws full trying to keep the goldfish and the canary safe from harm.

When Aunt Sarah saw the terrible mess, she was sure it was all Lady's fault.

"You naughty dog!" Aunt Sarah scolded as she chased Lady from the house with a broom.

Poor Lady. She had never been so insulted in all her life! Upset, she walked out of the yard. Lady didn't pay attention to where she was going, just as long as it was as far from Aunt Sarah as possible.

It wasn't long before Lady found herself on the other side of town.  She was far from her home and the well-mannered dogs who were her friends.

Suddenly Lady heard the angry growls of a pack of vicious dogs. To her surprise, they began to chase her! But before they could harm Lady, Tramp showed up to save the day.

"Why don't you pick on somebody your own size,
instead of bothering the lady!" Tramp shouted at the
pack of dogs.

Tramp fought like a tiger, and when he was through,
those bullies couldn't run away fast enough!

Lady thanked Tramp for rescuing her. Then she told
him all about her troubles with Aunt Sarah and the
wicked cats.

"Poor Pidge," said Tramp. "How about a nice, hot meal to cheer you up?" he suggested. He brought Lady to the best Italian restaurant in town.

"What a nice surprise!" cried Tony, the chef, when Tramp appeared at the back door.

Tony was so delighted to see Tramp with such a lovely lady that he brought out a big plate of spaghetti and meatballs for the two dogs to share. He even serenaded them with his accordion!

"This is wonderful!" Lady said to herself. She gazed fondly at Tramp. "He's not so bad after all, even if he doesn't have a collar."

After dinner, Tramp took Lady for a romantic stroll through the park.

That night,
the two dogs fell
asleep under
a full moon.

"Oh dear!" cried Lady the next morning. "I should have been home hours ago."

"Aw, forget about the rules for once," replied Tramp. "There's a whole big world out there for us to explore."

"But who will watch over the baby?" asked Lady.

"You win," said Tramp. "I'll take you home."

Their walk was quite pleasant until Tramp spotted a henhouse. His eyes lit up at once.

"Chickens!" he cried. "Ever chase chickens, Pidge? It's fun!"

Before Lady could stop him, Tramp ran into the midst of the clucking hens.

"Stop!" shouted Lady.

But Tramp was having too much fun to stop—until the owner of the henhouse called the dogcatcher.

"Run, Lady, run!" called Tramp as he sped away. He thought Lady was right behind him.

But Lady wasn't fast enough. As she rounded a corner, the dogcatcher nabbed her and threw her into his wagon! Tramp had no idea what had happened to her.

Before she knew it, Lady was behind bars at the city pound. She was so ashamed!

"What are you in for, sweetheart?" laughed Bull, the bulldog. "Putting fleas on the butler?"

Luckily, a kind dog named Boris told Lady that she had nothing to fear. "Dogs with name tags never stay here long," he explained.

Sure enough,
early the next
morning one of
the guards came
for Lady and took
her home.

But Aunt Sarah was still upset, so she chained Lady up outside.

Soon Tramp, who had been searching for Lady all night, came prancing into her yard.

"Pidge!" he exclaimed happily. "I've been so worried!"

"Don't call me Pidge!" snapped Lady. "This is all your fault. I never want to see you again."

Lady felt sad and lonely. She had promised Darling that she would protect the baby. But how could she do her job if she was chained up outside?

Soon it was dark. Lady tossed and turned, but she could not fall asleep. Suddenly she noticed something moving. It was a huge rat, and it was heading straight for the house!

Lady watched
in terror as the rat
climbed to the roof
and through the
baby's window.

"Woof! Woof!
Woof!" she cried.

Tramp came
running when he
heard her bark.

"A rat!" cried
Lady. "In the
baby's room!"

Tramp rushed
into the house.
Lady managed to
break her chain
and follow him.

Together, they
ran to the baby's room.

Tramp quickly
pounced on the rat,
and they began
to fight!

Tramp and the rat rolled around on the floor, knocking over lamps and chairs. Finally, though, Tramp won.

"Waa! Waa! Waa!" wailed the baby, who was frightened by all the noise.

Aunt Sarah was awakened by the baby's cries. "Shoo!" she cried. "Get back, you brute! Down to the cellar with you!"

Aunt Sarah wasted no time in calling the dogcatcher.
And for the first time in his life, Tramp found himself on
his way to the pound. Lady watched sadly as the wagon
pulled away.

Just then, Jim Dear and Darling arrived home.

"What's going on here?" asked Jim Dear.

"I found a stray dog in the baby's room," explained Aunt Sarah. "And your dog, here, was right beside him."

With that, Lady began to bark and headed up the stairs.

"Stop her!" squealed Aunt Sarah. "She'll hurt the baby!"

"Nonsense," Jim Dear replied. "She's trying to tell us something."

Lady led
them all to the
dead rat that lay
hidden behind
the chair in the
baby's room.

"Merciful heavens!" exclaimed Aunt Sarah.
"Good dog!" said Jim Dear, giving Lady a hug. "You
did your job well, girl, just as I knew you would."

"But what about that other dog?" asked Jim Dear.
"He was brave, too. Let's see if we can stop the
dogcatcher before he gets to the pound."

Jim Dear and Lady hurried outside. Then they hopped
into a taxi and sped after the dogcatcher's wagon.

When they finally caught up with the wagon, Jim Dear explained to the dogcatcher that Tramp didn't belong in the pound.

"You really like this tough guy, don't you?" Jim Dear asked Lady. "Well, why don't we invite him to come and live with us," he added.

Lady smiled at Tramp. Then she wagged her tail to let Jim Dear know she thought this was a splendid idea.

It took some getting used to, but Tramp grew to love being part of a family. Jim Dear and Darling grew to love him, too. It wasn't long before he had a collar and name tag of his own.

When Christmas Eve rolled around again, Lady and
her Tramp had some very special presents under the
tree—not one, not two, not even three, but four
adorable puppies of their very own.